Dear Parent:
Your child's love of reading starts here!

Every child learns to read in a different way and at his or her own speed. Some go back and forth between reading levels and read favorite books again and again. Others read through each level in order. You can help your young reader improve and become more confident by encouraging his or her own interests and abilities. From books your child reads with you to the first books he or she reads alone, there are I Can Read Books for every stage of reading:

SHARED READING
Basic language, word repetition, and whimsical illustrations, ideal for sharing with your emergent reader

BEGINNING READING
Short sentences, familiar words, and simple concepts for children eager to read on their own

READING WITH HELP
Engaging stories, longer sentences, and language play for developing readers

READING ALONE
Complex plots, challenging vocabulary, and high-interest topics for the independent reader

ADVANCED READING
Short paragraphs, chapters, and exciting themes for the perfect bridge to chapter books

I Can Read Books have introduced children to the joy of reading since 1957. Featuring award-winning authors and illustrators and a fabulous cast of beloved characters, I Can Read Books set the standard for beginning readers.

A lifetime of discovery begins with the magical words "I Can Read!"

Visit www.icanread.com for information
on enriching your child's reading experience.

I Can Read Book® is a trademark of HarperCollins Publishers.

Dixie and the Big Bully. Copyright © 2013 by HarperCollins Publishers. All rights reserved. Printed in the United States of America. No part of this book may be used or reproduced in any manner whatsoever without written permission except in the case of brief quotations embodied in critical articles and reviews. For information address HarperCollins Children's Books, a division of HarperCollins Publishers, 10 East 53rd Street, New York, NY 10022.
www.icanread.com

Library of Congress catalog card number: 2012939321
ISBN 978-0-06-208637-2 (trade bdg.) —ISBN 978-0-06-208621-1 (pbk.)

12 13 14 15 16 LP/WOR 10 9 8 7 6 5 4 3 2 1 ❖   First Edition

Dixie
and the
BIG BULLY

story by Grace Gilman

pictures by Sarah McConnell

HARPER

An Imprint of HarperCollinsPublishers

Dixie was walking Emma
to school.

"Fire, fire!"
shouted a girl named Becky.

"Where?" said Emma.

She looked all around.

"It wasn't a fire after all,"

said Becky.

"It was only your red hair!"

Becky laughed

and so did Becky's friends.

Emma did not laugh.

It wasn't funny to her.

"I wish you could stay with me,"

Emma said to Dixie.

"I need a friend today."

Emma sighed.

"Go home now, Dixie," she said.

"I'll see you after school."

Dixie didn't want to go home.

She wanted to stay at school.

Emma needed a friend.

Dixie waited for the doors to open.

She slipped inside the school.

Dixie found Emma.

"No dogs in the classroom, Emma!"

said the teacher.

"Pssst, Emma," Becky hissed.

"Did your dog eat your homework?"

Emma sent Dixie home.

But Dixie didn't go.

She slipped back into the school.

But this time

Dixie hid in the janitor's closet.

Dixie waited there for a long time.

She wanted to be close to Emma.

She knew Emma needed a friend.

Then the school bell rang.

Dixie jumped.

Things fell.

Someone heard the noise

and opened the door.

Dixie was sure it was Emma.

She barked.

She jumped.

But she was wrong.

It wasn't Emma.

It was a mess.

Stuff fell everywhere.

Bottles rolled on the floor.

Papers flew in the air.

And a mop fell on Becky's head.

Everyone saw, and everyone laughed.

Everyone, that is, except Becky.

"What are you looking at?"
Becky said.
"It's no fun being laughed at,
you know."

Emma nodded.

"I know," she said.

"Now I bet you'll start calling me
Mop Top," Becky said.
She looked sad.

"No, I won't," Emma said.

Becky smiled.

"Thanks," she said softly.

"I'm sorry I made fun of you, Emma,"
Becky said.

"I was just trying to be funny."

"It wasn't funny to me,"
Emma said.

"I see that now," Becky said.

Becky started to pick everything up.
Emma saw that all of Becky's friends
had already left.

"Dixie," Emma whispered,

"I think Becky needs a friend today."

Dixie ran over and licked Becky.

"Hey!" Becky said.

She smiled at Emma.

"Does this mean we're friends?"

she asked.

"Friends," Emma said.

Dixie howled.

Emma smiled.

"And that means

Dixie wants to be friends, too!"